Dear Mrs LaRue

tters from Obedience School

Written and Illustrated by

Mark Teague

The Snort City

September 30

For Tracy Mack, Brilliant Editor;
David Saylor, Impeccable Designer; and Earl and Ali, Dogs of Genius

Scholastic Children's Books
Commonwealth House, 1-19 New Oxford Street
London WC1A 1NU, UK
a division of Scholastic Ltd
London ~ New York ~ Toronto ~ Sydney ~ Auckland
Mexico City ~ New Delhi ~ Hong Kong

First published in the USA by Scholastic Inc., 2002
This paperback edition first published in the UK by Scholastic Ltd, 2003

Copyright © Mark Teague, 2002

ISBN 0 439 97716 9

LOCAL DOG ENTERS OBEDIENCE SCHOOL

"Ike"
LaRue

Citing a long list of behavioural problems, Snort City resident Gertrude R. LaRue yesterday enrolled her dog, Ike, in the Igor Brotweiler Canine Academy. Established in 1953, the Academy has a history of dealing with such issues.

"I'm at my wits' end!" said Mrs LaRue. "I love Ike, but I'm afraid he's quite spoiled. He steals food right off the kitchen table, chases the neighbour's cats, howls whenever I'm away, and last week while I was crossing the street he pulled me down and tore my best camel hair coat! I just don't know what else to do!"

Academy officials were unavailable for comment. . .

Dear Mrs LaRue,

October 1

How could you do this to me? This is a PRISON, not an academy! You should see the other dogs. They are BAD DOGS, Mrs LaRue! I do not fit in. Even the journey here was a nightmare. I am very unhappy and may need something to chew on when I get home. Please come right away!

Sincerely,
Ike

Dear Mrs LaRue,

Were you really so upset about the chicken pie? You know, you might have discussed it with me. You could have said, "Ike, don't eat the chicken pie. I'm saving it for dinner." Would that have been so difficult? It would have prevented a lot of hard feelings. Needless to say, I am being horribly mistreated. You say I should be patient and accept that I'll be here for a term. Are you aware that a term lasts TWO MONTHS? Do you know how long that is in dog years?

Sincerely,
Ike

October 3

Dear Mrs LaRue,

I'd like to clear up some misconceptions about the Hibbins' cats. First, they are hardly the little angels Mrs Hibbins makes them out to be. Second, how should I know what they were doing out on the fire escape in the middle of January? They were being a bit melodramatic, don't you think, the way they cried and refused to come down? It's hard to believe they were really sick for three whole days, but you know cats.

Your dog,
Ike

Sit

GRUESOME PRISON TALES ||||

October 4

Dear Mrs LaRue,

You should see what goes on around here. The way my teach— I mean WARDEN, Miss Klondike, barks orders is shocking. Day after day I'm forced to perform the most meaningless tasks. Today it was "sit" and "roll over", all day long. I flatly refused to roll over. It's ridiculous. I won't do it. Of course I was SEVERELY punished.

And another thing: who will help you cross the street while I'm away? You know you have a bad habit of not looking both ways. Think of all the times I've saved you. Well, there was that one time, anyway. I must say you weren't very grateful, complaining on and on about the tiny rip in your ratty old coat. But the point is, you need me!

Yours,
Ike

Dear Mrs LaRue,

October 5

The GUARDS here are all caught up in this "good dog, bad dog" thing. I hear it constantly: "Good dog, Ike. Don't be a bad dog, Ike." Is it really so good to sit still like a zombie all day? Nevertheless, I refuse to be broken! Miss Klondike has taken my typewriter. She claims it disturbs the other dogs. Does anybody care that the other dogs disturb ME?

Yours,
Ike

Dear Mrs LaRue,

Were the neighbours really complaining about my howling? It is hard to imagine. First, I didn't howl that much. You were away those nights, so you wouldn't know, but trust me, it was quite moderate. Second, let's recall that these are the same neighbours who are constantly waking ME up in the middle of the afternoon with their loud vacuuming. I say we all have to learn to get along.

My life here continues to be a nightmare. You wouldn't believe what goes on in the cafeteria.

Sincerely,
Ike

P.S. I don't want to alarm you, but the thought of escape has crossed my mind!

October 6

50 GREAT ESCAPES

Menu
APPETIZERS=
"FLOOR-DROPPED" TABLE SCRAPS
a Brotweiler Specialty
GOLDEN CHEWY BONE
with gravy.
ENTREES=
ROAST

October 7

Dear Mrs LaRue,

I hate to tell you this, but I am terribly ill. It started in my paw, causing me to limp all day. Later I felt queasy, so that I could barely eat dinner (except for the Yummy gravy). Then I began to moan and howl. Finally, I had to be taken to the vet. Dr Wilfrey claims that he can't find anything wrong with me, but I am certain I have an awful disease. I must come home at once.

Honestly Yours,
Ike

October 8

Dear Mrs LaRue,

Thank you for the lovely get well card. Still, I'm a little surprised that you didn't come get me. I know what Dr Wilfrey says, but is it really wise to take risks with one's health? I could have a relapse, you know.

With autumn here, I think about all the fine times we used to have in the park. Remember how sometimes you would bring along a tennis ball? You would throw it and I would retrieve it EVERY TIME, except for once when it landed in something nasty and I brought you back a stick instead. Ah, how I miss those days.

Yours truly,
Ike

P.S. Imagine how awful it is for me to be stuck inside my tiny cell!
P.P.S. I still feel pretty sick.

October 9

Dear Mrs LaRue,

By the time you read this I will be gone. I have decided to attempt a daring escape! I'm sorry it has come to this, since I am really a very good dog, but frankly you left me no choice. How sad it is not to be appreciated! From now on I'll wander from town to town without a home — or even any dog food, most likely. Such is the life of a desperate outlaw. I will try to write to you from time to time as I carry on with my life of hardship and danger.

Your lonely fugitive,
Ike

The Snort City Register/Gazette

LARUE ESCAPES DOGGY DETENTION

Former Snort City resident Ike LaRue escaped last night from the dormitory at the Igor Brotweiler Canine Academy. The dog is described as "toothy" by local police. His current whereabouts are unknown.

"To be honest, I thought he was bluffing when he told me he was planning to escape," said a visibly upset Gertrude R. LaRue, the dog's owner. "Ike tends to be a bit melodramatic, you know. Now I can only pray that he'll come back." Asked if she would return Ike to Brotweiler Academy, Mrs LaRue said that she would have to wait and see. "He's a good dog basically, but he can be difficult. . ."

October 11 — Somewhere in America

Dear Mrs LaRue,

I continue to suffer horribly as I roam this barren wasteland. Who knows where my wanderings will take me now? Hopefully to some place with yummy food! Remember the special treats you used to make for me? I miss them. I miss our nice, comfy apartment. But mostly, I miss you!

Your sad dog,
Ike

P.S. I even miss the Hibbins' cats, in a way.

Dear Mrs LaRue,

The world is a hard and cruel place for a "stray" dog. You would scarcely believe the misery I've endured. So I have decided to return home. You may try to lock me up again, but that is a risk I must take. And frankly, even more than myself, I worry about you. You may not know it, Mrs LaRue, but you need a dog!

Your misunderstood friend,

Ike

HERO DOG SAVES OWNER!

Ike LaRue, until recently a student at the Igor Brotweiler Canine Academy, returned to Snort City yesterday in dramatic fashion. In fact he arrived just in time to rescue his owner, Gertrude R. LaRue of Second Avenue, from an oncoming truck. Mrs LaRue had made the trip downtown to purchase a new camel hair coat. Apparently she neglected to look both ways before stepping out into traffic.

The daring rescue was witnessed by several onlookers, including policeman Newton Smitzer. "He rolled right across two lanes of traffic to get to her," said Smitzer. "It was really something. I haven't seen rolling like that since I left the police academy."

Mrs LaRue was unhurt in the incident, though her coat was badly torn. "I don't care about that," she said. "I'm just happy to have my Ike back home where he belongs!"

LaRue said she plans to throw a big party for the dog. "All the neighbours will be there, and I'm going to serve Ike's favourite dishes. . ."

I LIKE IKE